Eric Carle
From Head to Toe

HarperCollinsPublishers

I am a penguin
and I turn my head.
            Can you do it?

I can do it!

I am a giraffe
and I bend my neck.
        Can you do it?

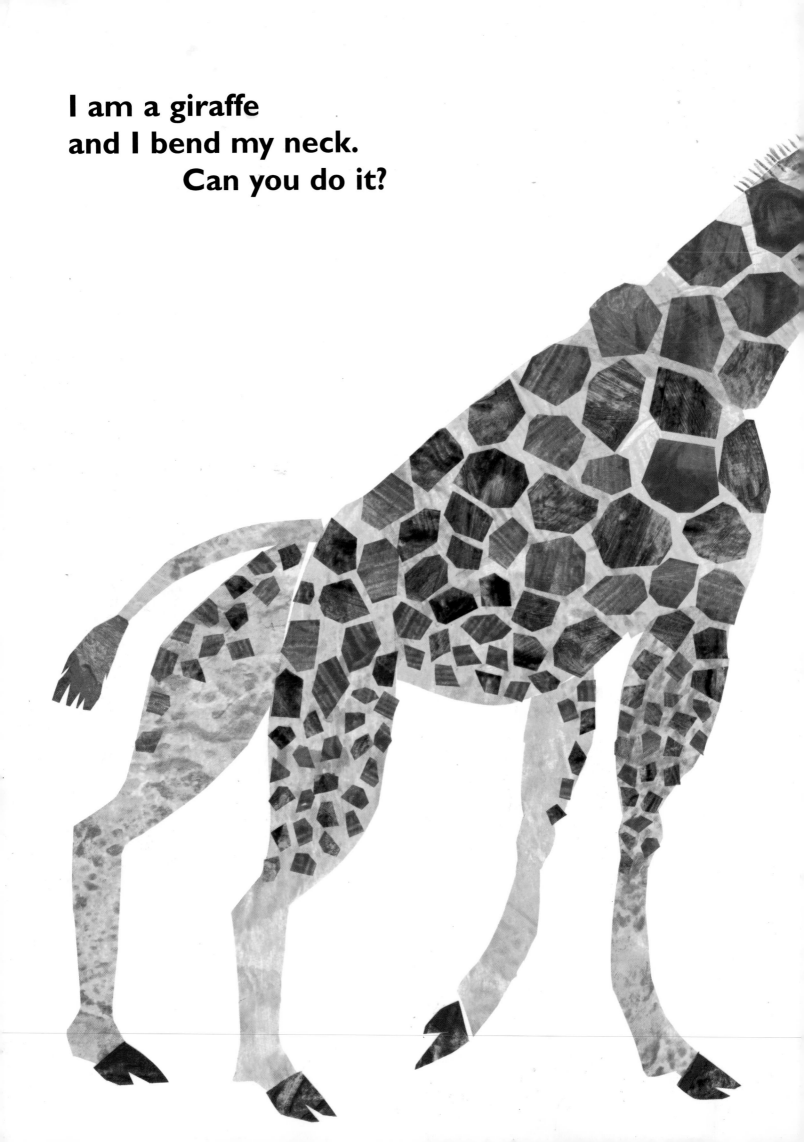

I can do it!

I am a buffalo
and I raise my shoulders.
   Can you do it?

I can do it!

I am a monkey
and I wave my arms.
  Can you do it?

I am a seal
and I clap my hands.
Can you do it?

I can do it!

I am a gorilla
and I thump my chest.
Can you do it?

I can do it!

I am a cat
and I arch my back.
Can you do it?

I can do it!

I am a crocodile
and I wriggle my hips.
Can you do it?

I can do it!

I am a camel
and I bend my knees.
Can you do it?

I can do it!

I am a donkey
and I kick my legs.
Can you do it?

I can do it!

I am an elephant
and I stomp my foot.
    Can you do it?

I can do it!

I am I
and I wiggle my toe.
        Can you do it?

I can do it! I can do it!